# TREASURE HUNTERS
# IN TROUBLE

# TREASURE HUNTERS IN TROUBLE

## AN UNOFFICIAL GAMER'S ADVENTURE BOOK FOUR

Winter Morgan

Sky Pony Press
New York

Copyright © 2015 by Hollan Publishing, Inc.

All rights reserved. No part of this book may be reproduced in any manner without the express written consent of the publisher, except in the case of brief excerpts in critical reviews or articles. All inquiries should be addressed to Sky Pony Press, 307 West 36th Street, 11th Floor, New York, NY 10018.

Sky Pony Press books may be purchased in bulk at special discounts for sales promotion, corporate gifts, fund-raising, or educational purposes. Special editions can also be created to specifications. For details, contact the Special Sales Department, Sky Pony Press, 307 West 36th Street, 11th Floor, New York, NY 10018 or info@skyhorsepublishing.com.

Sky Pony® is a registered trademark of Skyhorse Publishing, Inc.®, a Delaware corporation.

Minecraft® is a registered trademark of Notch Development AB. The Minecraft game is copyright © Mojang AB.

Visit our website at www.skyponypress.com.

10 9 8 7 6 5 4 3 2

Manufactured in Canada
This product conforms to CPSIA 2008

Library of Congress Cataloging-in-Publication Data is available on file.

Cover photo credit Megan Miller

Print ISBN: 978-1-63450-090-6
Ebook ISBN: 978-1-63450-091-3

# TABLE OF CONTENTS

# 1
# LOST FRIENDS

Steve was tending to his wheat farm when he heard his dog, Rufus, barking in the distance. He looked up to see two people approaching.

"Who are you?" Steve asked as he walked up to them. Rufus stood by his side, as his ocelots, Snuggles and Jasmine, sat by the entrance of his home.

At first the two people didn't say anything to Steve. They just looked at the house and talked to each other.

"Are you Steve?" the woman asked.

"Yes. Who are you?"

"Oh good, we found the right place. We weren't certain we would. It's been a crazy trip here," the woman sighed.

"You haven't told me who you are." Steve was getting annoyed.

"I'm sorry. I'm Alex and this is Will, but that's not important. I'm here to tell you that your friends are in trouble," Alex told him. She was a blonde woman wearing a green shirt.

"What? Who? How?" Steve blurted out, because this news bothered him greatly.

"I met your friend Kyra. She was trying to help her friends, who were trapped by a griefer. He had them trapped in a desert temple, but she was able to escape," said Alex.

"Are they okay? Where were you?"

"We met Kyra in the desert. We were starving and she gave us food. Kyra asked us to find you in return for the food. She didn't want to leave her friends, Henry, Max, and Lucy, but she needed your help," explained Will, who wore a red helmet.

Steve paused; he wondered if Alex and Will were telling the truth. They could be the griefers who had trapped his friends and were now here to steal from him.

"You traveled all the way from the desert to relay Kyra's message? That seems like a huge favor to ask of somebody."

Alex looked down as though she were embarrassed when she told Steve, "Kyra also promised to share some of the treasure with us."

"That makes sense," Steve reasoned.

"The temple is full of treasure," added Will.

"I'm worried about Kyra. I don't care about the treasure." Steve was upset.

"She has a tough job, but at least she can see hostile mobs more easily in the desert, because it's flat," explained Alex.

Steve knew that was true, and he also knew Kyra was smart and would be able to challenge the griefers, but she was only one person. Even if she saw all the hostile mobs that were about to attack her, it didn't mean she'd win. He had to help her! Steve went into his house and put on armor. He opened a chest and took out his diamond sword. He was ready to help Kyra save Henry, Max, and Lucy. He checked through his inventory to see if he had all the supplies he needed; the journey to the desert biome was a long and dangerous trip.

Alex and Will were in his living room, waiting for Steve, eating apples to increase their food bars.

"Do you have a map?" asked Steve.

"You don't need a map; we know the way, and we promised Kyra that we'd take you to her," replied Alex.

"But our inventories are almost empty," announced Will.

"What do you need?"

"We have lots of emeralds. Is there a village nearby? We can trade them and get supplies," suggested Alex.

"Yes, but do we have time? I'm worried about my friends. We need to hurry and save them."

"If we aren't prepared, we won't be able to save anyone," Alex lectured Steve.

Steve tried not to laugh; this sounded like something he would say. He had to agree with Alex. They needed to be prepared.

The trio walked toward the village to Eliot the Blacksmith's shop. He had all the supplies they needed to craft powerful swords and protective armor to battle these tricky griefers.

Eliot was surprised to see his friend Steve, and Steve's two new friends. "What can I help you with?"

"Eliot, this is Alex and Will. We are about to go to the desert. A griefer has trapped Henry, Lucy, and Max. Kyra is there trying to help them, but she can't do it alone."

"Oh no!" Eliot was upset. "Tell me what you need."

Alex and Will traded emeralds. When they were done, they rushed back to Steve's wheat farm and crafted all the items they needed to battle the many hostile mobs, but night was falling.

Steve walked outside. He was ready to start the trip. He didn't want to waste any more time.

Alex called after him. "We can't start our journey at night. We'll be killed within seconds!"

"Look behind you!" shouted Will.

*Click! Clang!* Two skeletons walked toward him. One shot an arrow at Steve, but it didn't graze his skin. With his armor on, he felt confident he'd win as he lunged toward a skeleton with his sword and destroyed it.

The other skeleton was harder to battle. As he struck the white bony creature, he found he couldn't destroy it. It was shooting arrows at him nonstop.

Will and Alex sprinted from the house and shot arrows at the skeleton until they destroyed it and it dropped arrows.

"We can use these skeleton bones for bonemeal," Alex said as she placed them in her inventory.

"See, it's too dangerous at night," insisted Will.

Steve knew they were right, but he couldn't sleep when he knew his friends were in trouble.

"I hope Kyra is okay," Steve told them as they walked into his house. Once they were in their beds, they'd be safe from the hostile mobs.

"A spider!" Alex screamed.

Its creepy red eyes glowed as it crawled across Steve's living room floor. Steve struck the insect with his diamond sword. The spider's eyes dropped out.

"We can use these to brew potions." Steve took the eyes as Alex picked up the string from the spider.

"Let's get into bed." Will was nervous. "There are too many hostile mobs."

As they made their way to the beds, Steve thought about Kyra. He hoped she'd be okay. He climbed into his bed, but then he heard a familiar voice come from the living room.

"Steve? Are you home?" the voice called out.

Steve jumped out of bed and sprinted to the living room.

"Kyra!" Steve saw his friend. "I thought you were in the desert!"

# 2
# RESPAWN

"It was a creeper." Kyra could barely get the words out. "I heard it, but I didn't have enough time to escape."

"That's awful!" exclaimed Steve. "But you're safe from creepers here. We have two ocelots."

"True. That creeper was a nightmare. The only good part was that I respawned in my bed, so I came over here to ask for your help," Kyra paused. "Did Alex and Will make it here? Did they tell you what happened?"

Steve started to explain, but Kyra interrupted him.

"Oh, Steve you won't believe what happened to Henry, Max, and Lucy."

At that point, Alex and Will emerged from the bedroom.

"Kyra?" Alex was shocked.

"You made it!" Kyra smiled.

"Yes, we were going to leave for the desert in the morning. What happened to you?" asked Alex.

"Did you give Steve my message?" asked Kyra.

"We told him how you were trying to help your friends who were trapped by a griefer," said Will.

"Steve, three rainbow-colored griefers trapped us."

"The rainbow men! I've seen them in the Nether and the jungle." Steve couldn't believe the rainbow griefers had struck again.

"We were just about to unearth the treasure when they snuck into the desert temple with diamond swords and trapped us."

"How?" Steve wondered why Henry, Max, and Lucy wouldn't be able to fight back. They were experienced treasure hunters who had encountered many griefers.

"At first we were so excited to find the hidden temple. When we found the room with the treasure, Henry was able to get around the booby traps, but he never destroyed the TNT. When the rainbow men came upon us, one of them stood by the TNT. He said he'd blow it up and kill us all if we didn't comply with their demands. The men led us to a bedrock room they must have built. Luckily, I was able to run away. I don't even think they noticed until it was too late."

"What was your plan to help Henry, Max, and Lucy escape?" asked Steve.

"I was going to try to steal the TNT and then use it to attack the griefers, but it was getting dark and there was a creeper—and now I'm here."

"We need to get back to the desert to help them. They could be trapped in there forever," Steve told Kyra.

Kyra walked over to Alex and Will. "Now that I have Steve, you don't have to come with us. I can reward you with some emeralds from my inventory. I can even give you one diamond each."

Alex looked at Will. "Would you mind if we still joined you?"

"Why?" Kyra seemed stunned.

Will said, "I think it would be an awesome adventure, and I know that desert temples have many treasures. They are one of the most valuable finds."

"We need all the help we can get. This isn't going to be easy," Steve told them.

"Oh no!" Out of nowhere, Kyra spotted a spider's red eyes.

Steve destroyed it with one blow. "This is the second one tonight. We must get into bed before a spider jockey or an Enderman attacks us. It's too dangerous to be out of our beds."

The door was still open. Steve went to close it, but two skeletons walked by, their bones creaking in the silent night.

"Get your bows and arrows ready!" Steve told the group as the skeletons shot arrows at the gang.

"What's that sound?" Kyra asked, her voice shaky.

A hissing sound grew louder.

"It sounds like a creeper!" shouted Steve.

"How could it be? You have two ocelots," Kyra stuttered.

"Stand back!" Will called out.

The skeletons killed the griefer. A music disc dropped on the floor. Steve and the gang shot arrows at the skeletons and destroyed them.

Steve picked up the disc and inspected it.

"This isn't the time to play music. We need to find our friends," Kyra reminded him as the sun rose in the distance.

The group walked out the door, ready to embark on the journey to save their friends from the griefer. They stopped when they saw another green, blocky, hostile mob slowly making its way toward them. Its four small legs made no noise as it moved closer.

"I don't understand. The sun's up. How could a creeper survive?" questioned Kyra.

"They can live in daylight. They're one of the only hostile mobs that can survive," Steve said as he slowly tried to walk away from the menacing creature, but it was pointless. There was no escape.

The group stood in fear. They braced themselves for an explosion. But then Snuggles and Jasmine walked toward the creeper and distracted the evil green devil from Steve and his friends.

"Run!" Steve shouted to his friends. They sprinted far from the wheat farm, starting their journey to save their friends trapped in the desert.

Just when they thought they were safe, only a short distance from Steve's farm, they encountered a swampy biome where the foursome stumbled upon a witch hut.

The small, black-hatted witch ran out of her hut with a bottle of potion.

The group had no means of escape. The witch charged at them and threw a potion on Steve. His body slowed down. He felt as though he couldn't move another step. He just wanted to fall to the ground and sleep.

"It's the potion of weakness!" Kyra called out in warning.

Despite knowing the potion's effects, Will raced toward the witch with his sword. He leapt at the witch, striking her. Witches were very strong and could regenerate, so the attack had no impact on her.

Steve needed help. Alex ran to him and handed him milk. "Drink this, it will make you feel better."

Steve drank the milk, but he felt awful and doubted that anything could help him.

Will battled the witch. He hit the lavender-eyed figure harder, but it didn't destroy her. She threw a potion at Will.

"I'm sick!" Will shouted as the potion of poison took away hearts on his health bar.

Kyra shot an arrow at the witch, destroying her.

"That's fantastic, Kyra!" Alex said as she gave Will milk.

Will drank as Steve walked over to him.

"It doesn't take very long, but you'll feel better," Steve reassured his new friend.

The group wanted to leave the swamp. They knew it was just a matter of time before they were attacked by the slimes that lived in that biome. But as they walked slowly through the marshy landscape, they could hear somebody call for help. Steve stopped.

"I know that voice!" Steve said, but he couldn't believe it.

# 3
# SURRENDER SLIME

**S**teve ran toward the voice. The potion of weakness had wiped him out, but the milk had worked; he was now happy to have energy.

"I'm here!" Steve called out. "Where are you?"

"Help!" The voice grew louder, so the group knew they were heading in the right direction.

Bats flew overhead and the sun was setting as they searched for the person screaming for help.

"We need to build a shelter. It's too dangerous to be outside at night. The swamp is a death trap," said Kyra.

Steve didn't pay attention. He was too focused on reaching the familiar voice. They sprinted along the water until they saw five green blocks hopping toward a person in the distance.

"Help!" the person called out once more.

Steve's instinct had been right! It was his friend Caleb from the building competition. "Caleb!" Steve screamed, "Don't worry! We'll help you!"

Caleb was surrounded by slimes that hopped toward him, ready to attack. Caleb's gold sword was no match for these slippery, slimy mobs.

"Steve!" Caleb was surprised to see his old friend.

"Caleb!" Kyra called out. "I'm here, too."

"Kyra! Please help me battle the slimes," Caleb said as he raced toward a large slime and struck it with his gold sword. When he hit it, it turned into two medium-sized slimes. It was a neverending battle. Caleb was able to destroy a mini slime and was left with slimeballs.

"Save the slimeballs!" Alex shouted, but Caleb was too busy battling the other slimes hopping at his feet to notice the slimeballs.

Steve joined Caleb, striking and defeating three large slime cubes with a single blow from his diamond sword.

Will, Alex, and Kyra fought alongside Steve, trying to stop this seemingly impossible battle of the slime.

*Squish! Squash!* The slimes hopped. No matter how many they destroyed, more seemed to spawn almost instantaneously.

"There must be a slime spawner over here. We need to find it!" Caleb told them.

"There could be a slime farm," added Kyra as she crashed her sword against a small slime. It disappeared and left a slimeball.

"I'll go look for the spawner," Steve told the group as they battled the bouncy beasts.

Steve stalked away from the swampy water. He knew that slimes couldn't swim, so the spawner would be farther inland. He came upon a small patch of land, thick with trees, and looked down to see a large hole. Steve peeked in his head and saw a tunnel with torches lighting the path. He was about to climb deeper into the hole, but stopped. He knew he couldn't do this alone. Steve quickly returned to the gang.

"There's a large hole in the ground. I think someone is spawning the slime down there!" Steve told them, and his friends rushed toward the tunnel, still trying to defeat the slime hopping around them.

Steve was the first person to climb down the tunnel. He held a torch as he led the group into the eerily silent tunnel.

"I don't see any slimes," Kyra remarked as she carefully made her way through the tunnel.

"And I don't hear any slimes," added Caleb.

"They have to be here." Steve couldn't imagine where else they'd be coming from. He also wondered who had built this tunnel and if they were still in the swamp biome.

A blur of colors raced past Steve and the gang.

"It's a rainbow griefer!" Kyra called out.

"Remember how Joshua used a rainbow griefer to destroy the building competition?" Caleb said as the group walked down the tunnel, closer to the griefer.

"Rainbow griefers have Henry, Max, and Lucy trapped in the desert. I don't think being in this tunnel is a good idea; they could trap us down here." Kyra wanted to leave.

"We're all nervous, Kyra, but we have to find out where these slimes are spawning or we won't be able to stop them," said Steve.

"But what if we are attacked by the rainbow griefer? Then we can never help our friends." Kyra didn't let the matter drop.

Alex defended Steve. "Steve's right. We have to get to the bottom of this slime problem."

They suddenly stopped when they heard a loud noise. *Squish! Squash!*

"It's the slime spawning room!" Steve was excited. "It must be right down this hall," he guessed.

The group made a right turn in the tunnel. Instead of entering a room filled with slime, they were stopped by a rainbow griefer wearing red armor and holding a brick of TNT.

"You walk one step closer and I'll blow up this tunnel!" the griefer shouted.

"But you'll destroy all of us," Steve pleaded, trying to reason with the griefer.

"Makes no difference to me. I live here, so I'll just respawn." The rainbow griefer laughed.

*Squish! Squash!* Three slimes hopped from the slime spawn room and leapt at the rainbow griefer, destroying him. Steve and the gang sprinted away. They wanted to be far away before he respawned.

The tunnel was longer than they remembered, and it felt as though they'd never reach the end. When they finally saw light peeking through the hole above them, they climbed up a makeshift ladder made of vines and made their escape. Emerging in the evening light, a bat flew close to their heads.

"We're safe! Let's get out of here!" Will shouted, but he had spoken too soon.

In the distance, the rainbow griefer sprinted toward the group, and although he didn't have a block of TNT, he was carrying a diamond sword.

The group tried to escape, but the rainbow griefer was fast. He caught up to them and leapt at Steve. The sword struck Steve's arm.

"Ouch!" Steve cried, as he lost hearts in his health bar.

Caleb shot an arrow at the griefer and struck him right in the chest. The griefer was weakened. Steve lunged at the rainbow man with his diamond sword, pounding him with his powerful enchanted sword. The rainbow griefer sprinted away. They knew the battle was far from over. There were rainbow griefers lurking all around the Overworld, and they had just begun their war on the rainbow ruffians.

*Squish! Squash!* The sound of slimes was emanating from the tunnel.

"We need to get out of the swamp!" Alex cried to the gang.

Steve picked up a large rock and covered the hole in the ground. "That should keep the slimes away for a while."

Night had fallen. They were stuck in the swamp. The group could make out two pairs of purple eyes in the dark sky.

"How are we going to escape?" Alex whispered.

"Swim!" Steve said, hopping into the murky swamp water filled with lily pads. The group followed.

# 4

# VIEWS AND VILLAINS

The sun rose, but the mountain's peak kept it hidden. The group was far from the swamp but surrounded by large hills, caves, and enormous mountains.

"It's so beautiful here," Kyra said as she stared at a waterfall at the top of a mountain.

Alex had made her way to the top and was about to walk down.

"Careful!" Steve called out. "You have to watch out. The other side is very steep, you can just fall off. There's no place to climb down."

"What should we do?" asked Will.

"We can just head back the way we came," suggested Alex.

"That's not a plan. That's how you get killed by a rainbow griefer," said Kyra.

"Do you guys know parkour?" asked Caleb.

"You mean jumping from mountain to mountain?" Kyra asked, her voice shaky.

"That sounds scary." Will looked at the mountaintop that they would need to reach to make their way across this mountainous biome.

"It's not scary. It's fun!" Caleb assured them. "It can seem a bit hardcore at times, but it's the ultimate adventure!"

The group wasn't convinced. Steve looked at the other mountain, trying to evaluate how long he'd be in midair and how far he'd fall if he didn't make it.

"I've heard of parkour, but it always seemed a little risky," Steve said, looking down at the valley between the two mountains.

"Watch me!" Caleb sprinted and jumped to the adjacent mountain. He landed safely.

"Wow!" Kyra was in awe.

"It's not hard at all!" Caleb shouted. "Join me!"

Steve couldn't believe he was going first. He wanted to close his eyes, but he knew he had to pay attention. This was an adventure, but it wasn't as easy as Caleb made it seem. Steve sprinted, then he jumped. His feet were in midair. It was like flying but it only lasted a second. He landed on top of the mountain.

"See! You did it!" Caleb was excited. One by one, they sprinted and jumped to the other mountain.

"The views are incredible from up here!" Steve looked out at the mountains; they seemed so majestic. He wanted to jump from mountain to mountain.

"Let's jump to the other mountain," suggested Kyra.

"No, it's too far. Parkour only works if you're fairly close to the place you are jumping to. You don't want to fall down and get killed," Caleb told her.

"I can't believe I was so scared and I still had the best time," Steve told the group.

"I told you!" Caleb smiled.

Everyone stopped and took in the view. It was the type of view you wished you could spend hours just looking at, the type that would make you want to paint a picture. The group couldn't stay very long. It was going to take awhile to hike down the mountain, and they didn't want to spend another night without shelter. They were getting tired and hungry and needed to make their way to a home for the night.

Finally, the group was at the bottom of the mountain. As they made their way through a grassy valley, they stumbled upon an entrance to a cave.

"Should we go mining?" asked Will.

"It seems like a waste if we don't," replied Kyra. "We can get emeralds and maybe even diamonds."

"I know, but it's going to get dark soon. We have to find some shelter. I think mining will be very dangerous," Steve warned them.

"Dangerous? You just jumped from the top of one mountain to another. That was dangerous," Caleb said as he walked toward the cave.

Everyone followed Caleb into the cave. Steve put on his helmet, got his pickaxe from his inventory, and met the others in the cave.

"Look at how deep we can go," marveled Alex.

"I found emeralds!" Kyra called out.

"I think we're going to find diamonds soon," Will said as he mined deeper.

"I see a cave spider!" Steve cried out, and Alex sprinted over and slammed her sword at the spider.

"There are going to be a lot of cave spiders, Steve," Alex remarked. "We're in a cave."

The group gathered emeralds, gold, and iron.

"I told you this was worth it," Kyra said, holding up gold ingots.

"You were right," admitted Steve. "Look at all of these resources. I can't wait to trade them with Eliot the Blacksmith."

The group dug deeper into the mine.

"I see blue!" Kyra shouted.

"Where?" Alex followed Kyra.

"Look! Diamonds!" Kyra banged her pickaxe against the wall.

The group gathered the diamonds.

"This is fantastic!" said Will.

They worked fast to place as many diamonds as they could in their inventory before night fell.

"Hand everything over!" a deep voice echoed in the cave.

The group looked up to see three rainbow men pointing bows and arrows at them.

# 5
# PORTALS

"**D**on't shoot!" Steve called to the rainbow griefers. "Why should we listen to you?" a rainbow man shouted and shot an arrow at Steve.

Steve was hit, but he was still able to race toward the rainbow man with his diamond sword. Caleb ran after Steve.

*Clash!* Steve struck the rainbow man but shielded himself with his arrow. Caleb was able to strike the rainbow man, too. Kyra shot two arrows, which significantly weakened the rainbow man. Steve delivered the final blow, and the griefer was destroyed.

Yet the battle wasn't over. Two more rainbow men remained, and they were fierce.

One rainbow man was in a sword battle with Alex.

*Clang!* The battle was intensifying. The rainbow man was forcing Alex into an area of the cave filled with cave spiders.

"Help!" she cried.

Steve wanted to assist Alex, but he was looking for the cave spider spawner. The spiders were filling the walls of the cave, and soon they'd all be bitten. He had to stop them from spawning.

Alex tried to fight the rainbow man, but he was a skilled swordsman. Will shot an arrow at the rainbow griefer and hit him in the eye. Alex was able to strike him with the sword just as a cave spider bit his leg. He was able to escape though, and sprinted out of the cave.

Then there was only one rainbow man left, and he was aiming an arrow at Kyra. Steve tried to reason with him.

"Look at what happened to your friends! What do you want from us?" he asked.

The rainbow man didn't reply. Instead he took out a sword and lunged toward Steve.

Steve sprinted. As he raced through the cave, Steve unknowingly stepped on a pressure plate.

*Thump!* Steve landed in a spawner room surrounded by silverfish and spiders.

"Help me!" he screamed from the hole in the ground.

Kyra sprinted toward Steve. "The rainbow man is getting away!" she yelled to the others.

Alex chased the rainbow man. She hit him from behind, but he got away. Alex ran to Kyra to help Steve get out of the hole. When Alex looked down, she gasped.

Cave spiders and silverfish surrounded Steve, and no matter how many he was able to crush, he had no hope of survival unless he could destroy the spawner.

Will jumped into the hole and ripped his pickaxe into the silverfish spawner. He banged against it as hard as he could. It was almost impossible to break, but Will worked hard and demolished it. Steve stamped out cave spiders and made his way over to the cave spider spawner. He placed two torches beside the spawner to disable it.

"How do we get out of here?" asked Will.

"We're going to have to mine our way out," Steve replied as he banged his pickaxe into the wall.

Will joined Steve and the two pickaxed the wall of the spawning room.

"Are you okay?" asked Kyra.

There was no reply.

Kyra looked down. They were missing!

"They're not there," she told Alex and Caleb.

Alex didn't believe her and had to take a peek, too.

"Where could they have gone?" Alex was shocked.

Kyra jumped into the hole. Alex and Caleb followed.

The cave wall had been demolished, and they looked through the other side and saw a large hole.

"What's that?" asked Alex.

"It's a stronghold!" replied Kyra.

Alex had never seen one before.

"Steve . . . Will . . . Are you guys okay?" Kyra called out to them.

"Yes, we're in a stronghold. And I think the only way out is through the portal to the End." Steve's voice had a shaky tone. Kyra could tell he was nervous.

"I have Ender Pearls," Alex said and jumped down into the stronghold.

Steve thought it was odd that Alex was so eager to go to the End. Caleb followed Alex into the stronghold.

Kyra reluctantly followed. She had put in enough time slaying the Ender Dragon and she didn't want to travel to the End.

"Don't get so excited, Alex. We don't even know where the portal room is; this stronghold has so many rooms," Steve told her.

The group explored the stronghold. Steve placed a torch on the wall, and they made a left turn into a hallway leading to an abandoned jail cell with iron bars.

"I wonder who was kept prisoner in here?" Caleb asked the group.

"It's super creepy," remarked Kyra.

Will walked into the room.

"Don't shut the door. You don't want to get trapped," Alex said with a smile.

Will rushed out. "Could that really happen?" he asked.

"I'm not sure, but let's not take any chances," Steve replied as they made their way past the prison and to a staircase.

"Should we go downstairs?" Kyra asked the group.

"Yes!" replied Alex.

They walked down the cobblestone stairs, but they couldn't go any farther. The group stood in front of an iron door.

"We have to use a pickaxe," Steve said as he started to knock against the door with great force.

The others joined Steve. They needed to see what was on the other side of the door. Using all of their strength, they mined through the door.

As the door fell to the ground, Steve placed a torch to give the group light. Alex pushed her way to the front of the group and made a right turn down the hallway.

"Alex, where are you going?" Will followed Alex.

"Oh my!" Alex shouted in delight. "Look at this!"

The group walked into the room where Alex stood. The room was lined with bookshelves and cobwebs. It was a small single-level library. Steve broke a cobweb away from his face.

"A chest!" Kyra pointed out. It sat at the end of one of the large bookshelves. Kyra opened it carefully.

"What's in it?" asked Steve.

Kyra held an enchantment book. "I bet this can help us."

"That's cool," said Alex, "but I've heard there are rooms in a stronghold that contain real treasures."

"What types of treasure?" Will was excited.

"I've heard that, too, but strongholds are very large and we would have to find our way to one of those rooms," Steve told him.

"And the only way out of here is through the End," Alex said with a smile.

"That's nothing to smile about, Alex," Steve said. But nobody seemed to hear him. His words were lost when Kyra screamed, "I found treasure!"

# 6
# IT'S NOT AN ENDING

Kyra had climbed down a ladder placed outside the library and found a storeroom with a chest.

"Open it!" Will stood over Kyra.

"I can't wait to see what's in it," Alex looked at the chest.

Steve was walking down the ladder when Kyra opened it and screamed, "Saddles!"

"Wow," Steve exclaimed, "that's rare!"

"And there are five saddles in the chest. One for each of us." Kyra handed saddles to the rest of the group.

"You don't have to share," Alex told her. "You can keep them all to yourself."

Kyra looked at Alex, perplexed.

"Thanks, Kyra," Steve said when she handed him the saddle.

"Now when we encounter any animals, we can just put a saddle on them and we can ride them." Kyra put the saddle in her inventory.

"This is a great find," said Will. "But we still need to find our way out of here!"

The group walked into another hallway that seemed to go on forever. Steve was nervous about finding the portal room. He had little interest in returning to the End. Yet Alex seemed extremely excited about the prospect of slaying the Ender Dragon.

"When we get to the End, I have a plan. I am an expert at destroying the Ender Dragon. Nobody has to worry; I can get us out of there," Alex told them.

The group stopped at another door. This one was also made of iron. They used their pickaxes to knock down the door again. It was another storeroom. Alex ran to the chest.

"Gold ingots!" Alex called out and began to put them in her inventory.

"What about us?" Kyra asked her.

"I'm the one who found the chest," Alex replied.

"That's not how it works. We're in this together!" Kyra was angry.

"I thought you were partners with Will?" Steve asked her. "Aren't you used to sharing?"

Alex paused and then put the remaining gold ingots in her inventory.

"Will," Steve asked him, "how can you let her do this to you? To us? Does she act like this all the time?"

Will stuttered and could barely get his words out. "Alex is in charge."

"In charge?" Steve was dumbfounded.

"How? Why?" Kyra also didn't understand.

Steve also knew they were getting distracted. He had three friends trapped by rainbow griefers who needed his help and here he was wasting time with Alex and Will. But he also didn't want Will to be partnered with someone who wasn't doing the right thing and, he had to admit, he wanted those gold ingots.

"This is crazy. Everyone should get gold ingots," said Caleb.

"Give us our ingots," Kyra demanded.

"No!" Alex was adamant; she wasn't handing them over.

Steve wasn't going to give up. He even contemplated threatening Alex with his diamond sword, but instead he calmly said, "Kyra gave everyone a saddle when she found the saddles. It's the way it works when you are part of a team."

"I never said I was part of a team."

"But Alex, we're a team . . . right?" asked Will.

"It's different with us," Alex replied. "Can we all forget about it and move on? I want to find the End Portal and get out of the stronghold."

"No, we can't. Just give everyone their share of the ingots and we can go find the portal. How can I battle the Ender Dragon with somebody I can't trust?" Kyra told Alex.

"You're acting like a rainbow griefer," Will told her.

With that comment, Alex handed everyone gold ingots. "Are you guys happy now? I didn't realize we had to share everything. What a pain!"

Steve wondered what motivated Alex. At first she seemed to be so nice and helpful, but she was showing them a side of herself that he didn't like at all. Kyra was right—what was going to happen when they reached the End? He wasn't sure who he was more afraid of, the Ender Dragon or Alex.

Steve didn't have much time to think about this. Once they left the storeroom, they walked down a hallway and found a wooden door, which they easily opened. There was a stone pillar in the room with a fountain in the center. They searched the room, but it was empty.

"We could go on like this forever." Kyra was getting frustrated.

"I know! This seems so pointless," Caleb remarked.

"Come here!" Will shouted from outside the fountain room.

Will had found the End Portal. He stood by a silverfish spawner.

"Watch out!" Kyra called to Will.

"It doesn't work." He looked down at the spawner.

"No! Look behind you!" Kyra shouted.

Will turned around to see a skeleton lurking in the corner, its bow and arrow aimed at him.

Will turned and was hit by the arrow. He took a gold sword out of his inventory and, with all his strength, he leapt at the skeleton and tried to clobber it. The skeleton was dangerously close to the lava pool. As Will battled the skeleton, he almost fell in the lava.

"Help!" he called out.

Kyra, Caleb, and Steve sprinted over and joined Will in battle, moving the fight away from the lava. Meanwhile Alex took the Eyes of Ender and started to place them around the portal.

Steve looked over at Alex as he battled the skeleton. He could imagine her leaving without them, and they'd be trapped in the stronghold forever. With one final strike, he was able to push the skeleton into the lava pool and sprinted toward the portal.

Steve raced past sixteen iron bar windows until he reached Alex. She was about to place the final Eye of Ender.

"Quick, guys!" Steve called out to the others.

They sprinted over to the portal that was about to be activated.

"You can't stop us!" Steve shouted at Alex. "We're coming with you!"

"I wouldn't have it any other way," Alex smirked as she placed the last Eye of Ender on the portal. Steve and Alex transported to the End, leaving Kyra, Caleb, and Will in the stronghold.

# 7

# THE RETURN

"How could you do that to Will, Caleb, and Kyra?" Steve asked, but there was no time for her answer. No matter how he felt about Alex, they were standing alone on a floating platform made of obsidian, and they had to battle the Ender Dragon together or it would be the end of both of them.

"Watch out!" Steve warned Alex. "You don't want to fall into the void."

Alex was close to the edge. "I used all of my Ender Pearls to make it to the Eyes of Ender."

Steve took four Ender Pearls from his inventory and handed two to Alex. "Take these—we can use them to teleport together."

"Why are you being so nice to me?"

"The more important question is why were you being so mean to all of us? I'm being nice to you because I need help fighting the Ender Dragon. Yes, I helped slay it many times before, but I never did it on my own."

The two teleported toward the Ender Dragon, landing next to an obsidian pillar, and were immediately surrounded by Endermen.

"Do you see the Ender Dragon?" Steve asked as he looked up at the starless sky.

The Endermen crept toward Steve and Alex. One Enderman opened its mouth and shrieked. Steve struck the lanky hostile mob with his diamond sword. More Endermen walked toward them, ready to attack. Alex took out her sword and hit as many Endermen as she could destroy.

*Roar!* The winged beast flew past them and ate Ender Crystals.

"We need to destroy those Ender Crystals. It's the only way we can defeat the dragon," Steve told Alex.

"Everybody knows that, Steve," Alex said. She shot an arrow at the Ender Crystals and they exploded.

The Ender Dragon swept close to the ground, almost hitting Alex and Steve.

"Good job, Alex." Steve was upset. "Now the Ender Dragon knows we're here."

"It was just a matter of time. Did you plan on hiding forever?" Alex asked as she shot an arrow at the dragon. It hit the dragon's belly, but the beast ate Ender Crystals placed on a pillar.

Steve was too busy trying to defeat the neverending army of Endermen to help Alex fight the dragon.

"Steve, you're not helping me at all!" she called out.

"Now you need my help?" he asked with an attitude. "I'm taking care of the Endermen," Steve said as he hit two of the mobs, obliterating them.

The Ender Dragon charged at the two and hit Alex.

"Are you okay?" Steve asked.

"My health bar is low. I don't know how I can battle the dragon anymore."

Steve took out a potion of healing from his inventory and handed it to Alex. "Maybe this can help."

"Thanks," Alex said as she took the potion.

Steve shot another arrow at the dragon and then aimed for the Ender Crystals the dragon was about to eat.

Bull's-eye. The crystals were destroyed.

"Making progress," Steve said as he shot another arrow at the flying menace.

Alex slowly regained her strength and shot arrows at the dragon.

"I think we can do it!" she said as she fought alongside Steve.

The dragon flew at them again, this time faster and with more force. Steve and Alex were able to move out of the way.

More Endermen were walking toward them under the dimly lit sky. Steve prepared to battle them. He took out a sword from his inventory and put away the bow and arrow.

"I have another plan!" Alex took snowballs from her inventory.

"Snowballs!" Steve was shocked.

"Bet you didn't think I had these on me. They work really well on the Ender Dragon," Alex said and threw one at the dragon. The snowball hit the dragon's side.

"Wow, that's amazing!" Steve said, seeing the dragon's health bar diminish. "They really do work."

Alex took out another snowball and handed it to Steve. "Try it," she said.

Steve swung his arm and threw the snowball as fast as he could, and the white icy snowball hit the dragon's face. It roared.

"You're making it angry," Alex said. She threw another ball at the dragon and handed another one to Steve.

Steve threw it at the dragon with all of his might and it struck the belly of the beast. Steve couldn't believe Alex was letting him throw her snowballs. This was a big difference from the way she had acted in the stronghold. But he couldn't rejoice, because the Endermen were getting closer.

Steve slayed the Endermen with his diamond sword as Alex threw snowballs at the dragon.

"Here." Alex gave him another snowball.

The dark and dreary landscape of the End was filled with winter's favorite weapon, the snowball.

"This is kind of fun." Steve felt bad admitting this to Alex.

"Look," Alex said as she pointed to an obsidian pillar. "There's the last Ender Crystal! Hit it!"

Steve took out his bow and arrow and hit the crystal. There was another explosion.

The snowballs were weakening the dragon. Its health bar was almost gone. Steve hit the dragon with an arrow. Then Alex threw a snowball. The Ender Dragon exploded. A dragon egg dropped and the two sprinted toward the portal to the Overworld.

When they emerged through the portal, familiar voices could be heard in the distance. They looked out at the landscape and couldn't believe where the portal had brought them.

# 8
# NETHER AGAIN

"Snuggles!" Steve sprinted toward his ocelot and saw Rufus and Jasmine walking toward him.

"The wheat farm!" Alex was shocked. "How did we wind up here?"

Kyra stood eating an apple. She offered an apple to Alex. Steve and Alex didn't realize how hungry they were and how low their food bars were after fighting the Ender Dragon.

"I guess you guys slayed the Ender Dragon," said Kyra.

"How did you guys wind up here?" Steve asked Kyra and Will.

"Right after you left, we were attacked by a spider jockey. It took us by surprise," replied Will.

"Just one?" questioned Alex.

"Yes, but we all had very low health and food bars. It didn't take much to wipe the group out. We respawned here," explained Will.

"Where's Caleb?" asked Steve.

"I assume he respawned wherever he slept last," said Kyra. "I hope we see him again."

"Me, too," said Will.

The group gathered in Steve's living room. Night was setting and they needed their energy for their second attempt to travel to the desert.

"I can't believe we had to start all over again. This is so annoying. I'm really worried about Henry, Max, and Lucy," Steve said as he paced back and forth.

"Well there's nothing we can do about it now. We need to get rest, and tomorrow we can start our trip to the desert," said Kyra.

Will looked at the map. "I have an idea. If we go to the Nether, we can get to the desert and we won't have to go through the swamp and the mountains."

"The Nether," said Kyra. "Ugh, I hate the Nether."

"Nobody likes the Nether," added Steve.

"I don't mind it," Alex smiled.

Two pairs of purple eyes crept past Steve's window.

"We need to get to bed. It's too dangerous to be in here," Steve told them. The group walked to the bedroom and got in their beds.

"You never told us how you slayed the Ender Dragon," Kyra said from her bed.

"Snowballs," replied Alex. "Steve and I did it together."

The group slept. When they awoke in the morning light, Steve filled up his inventory with potions and food.

"We need to be prepared," Steve informed them. "I know we've all been to the Nether before, but it's always a challenge."

The gang gathered outside the house and began to work on the frame for the Nether portal. They used obsidian to build four corners.

"Who has flint and steel?" asked Steve.

Alex took some out of her inventory and made a fire to activate the portal. "This time we're all going together," Alex said as they gathered in the portal. The portal made a loud, creepy sound and omitted purple mist. They were on their way to the red lava–filled land-scape of the Nether.

Within seconds of their arrival, two white ghasts with their eyes and mouths closed flew past them.

"Oh good, they don't see us," said Will.

One ghast opened its evil red eyes and shrieked.

"You spoke too soon!" Steve cried out and grabbed his bow and arrow.

The ghast shot a fireball at Steve. The flaming ball sped through the sky. Steve shot an arrow at the ball, deflecting it as it raced back toward the ghast.

*Boom!* The ghast exploded.

The other ghast made a loud noise, aiming a fireball at Alex. Steve jumped in front of Alex, shooting at the ball and again deflecting it to hit the ghast.

*Ka-boom!* The second ghast was destroyed.

"I can't believe we've only been here a minute and we've already been attacked by ghasts," remarked Kyra. "I told you I hate the Nether."

Will looked out across a sea of lava. "I think I see a Nether fortress."

"It could have treasure!" Alex was excited.

"What about the map?" Steve questioned. "I want to find my friends."

"Maps don't work in the Nether, remember?" replied Alex.

"That's right." Steve was upset. "How are we going to find our way?"

"It's fine," Will reassured him. "If we make it to the Nether fortress, we can create a portal over there and get back to the Overworld, and then we shouldn't be too far from the desert."

"If we make it to the Nether fortress," Kyra repeated.

The gang walked slowly through the netherrack ground, stopping by a lava waterfall.

"I hate to admit it," Kyra said, "but the waterfall is kind of pretty."

The group agreed as they carefully avoided getting any lava on them. They didn't want to wind up on the wheat farm, having to start the journey for a third time.

Glowstone blocks that grew on the underside of the netherrack landscape lit the dim skies in the Nether. They watched for the many lava pools they walked past on their trip to the Nether fortress.

"Look, we're almost there," Kyra said as the Nether fortress stood just a few feet away from them.

The group began to walk very slowly. "What's happening?" asked Kyra.

Steve looked down to see a patch of soul sand, which affected people by making them move at a much slower pace. "Look down, guys," he told them.

"We should use this to grow Nether wart," said Will.

"No, we don't have time. We have to avoid this patch, so we can sprint to the Nether fortress. Our friends are trapped," said Steve.

The group sped up when they were far away from the soul sand, and soon they were just inches from the entrance to the Nether fortress.

"Go in," Alex demanded as Will stood in front of the entrance.

"Will!" Steve shouted. "Look out!"

Four zombie pigmen walked toward Will, and he struck one with his sword, battling it until he defeated it.

Steve lunged at a zombie pigman with his sword.

"Alex, help!" Steve called out. He was struck by the zombie pigman and his health bar was low.

She sprinted over and struck the pigman with her sword until she destroyed it and saved Steve.

When the zombie pigmen were destroyed, they dropped gold nuggets. Alex picked one up and handed it to Steve.

Then two ghasts flew down. One shot a fireball at Will. He dodged the fireball, and it struck the zombie pigmen.

"We just have one more to destroy," Kyra said breathlessly.

"And two ghasts," Will added with an exhausted sigh.

There was no time to talk. It was all action. A fireball came toward the group. Steve shot an arrow at it and destroyed another ghast.

*Boom!*

Alex shot an arrow at the other ghast and it exploded. A ghast tear dripped down, but they couldn't catch it.

"That's so annoying," Alex said. "We could have made a regeneration potion with that tear."

Kyra battled the last zombie pigman using all her strength and her mighty diamond sword, and she was able to defeat the hostile mob. The group could finally enter the grand yet slightly creepy Nether fortress.

The fortress made of nether bricks had a large open area with a staircase and patches of soul sand growing near it.

"We need to find the treasure chest," Alex said as she explored the indoor rooms of the fortress. "It has to be here somewhere."

Will called out, "I think I found it!"

Will had found a room with a chest. But the room wasn't empty. A pair of orange-and-yellow eyes glowed in the corner of the dark room.

# 9
# LOOT AND LAVA

"It's a magma cube!" Kyra shouted.

Will hit the cube with his sword and it broke into four smaller cubes. The group descended upon the cubes and crushed them.

"Let's get the treasure!" Alex went to open the treasure chest.

"Be careful," warned Steve, "it might be booby-trapped."

But it was too late. Alex had already opened the chest, though luckily it wasn't rigged.

"Diamonds!" she showed the group.

They crowded around the chest. "Wow, there are gold swords," Kyra exclaimed as she looked in the chest.

"What a find," Steve said as he saw gold and iron ingots in the chest. "We have to empty it and split the loot."

The group took all the riches and then sprinted out of the temple. They now needed to make a portal back to the Overworld.

They didn't get very far. An evil beast with yellow skin and black eyes flew past them. Then another.

"Blazes!" Steve shouted.

Will stood by a doorway and screamed, "There's a blaze spawner in this room!"

"We must destroy it," Alex called out as she threw a snowball at the blaze, obliterating it.

Alex armed the group with snowballs. "These will destroy these monsters. I need to deactivate the spawner."

She sprinted into the room with the spawner as the gang threw countless snowballs at the many blazes that flew through the Nether fortress.

As the blazes were destroyed, they dropped glow-stone dust.

"We need to collect this glowstone dust. It will help us when we brew potions," Steve told them.

"How can we concentrate on collecting glowstone dust when we have to destroy the blazes?" asked Kyra while she threw a snowball at a blaze that dropped glow-stone dust.

Alex emerged from the room, "I did it. I deactivated the spawner."

"Fantastic," said Steve. "Let's get out of here."

They sprinted past the stairs with its patches of soul sand and nether wart. They sprinted past the empty rooms of the grand fortress until they were out of the fortress.

When they finally exited the fortress, they were met by another enemy.

"Not again!" Will cried out as two rainbow men sprinted toward them.

"We know you have treasure," one of the rainbow men yelled at them. "Hand it over!"

"Never!" Alex screamed to the griefers.

One of the rainbow men shot an arrow at Steve and it struck him. His health bar was dangerously low. If he was hit one more time, he'd be back on his wheat farm with Snuggles, Rufus, and Jasmine. He wanted to make it to the desert. He wanted to save his friends.

Alex rushed to Steve's side as the others battled the rainbow men. She took a potion of healing from her inventory and gave it to him. His health bar was restored.

"Thank you," said Steve.

"No problem. Now I want you to help me destroy these evil rainbow griefers. They're not taking any of our treasure."

Alex and Steve ran toward the rainbow griefers.

Will had cornered one of the rainbow men by a lava pool. The rainbow man was trying not to fall in. Steve sprinted toward the rainbow man, and the griefer lost his balance and fell into the lava.

"Gothca," Will said and he went to join the others battle against the other evil griefer.

Two wither skeletons approached the group dueling the rainbow man and began to strike them with stone swords, hitting Alex and Will.

Steve sprinted toward the skeletons with his diamond sword. Kyra shot arrows at the skeletons.

The wither skeletons distracted the group and the rainbow man was able to escape into the Nether.

The gang was too busy battling the wither skeletons to worry about the rainbow man. At least they still had their loot. They didn't want to lose any treasure; they had worked too hard and come too far to lose the battle.

Steve struck the wither skeleton hard and finally destroyed it. Kyra shot a final arrow that destroyed the other wither skeleton. The battle had been won.

"I don't think we saw the last of that rainbow griefer," Alex said as she looked into the distance.

"I just want to get out of the Nether. There are too many hostile mobs here and no real places to hide. It's a death trap," remarked Steve.

"Let's make a portal," Will said and the group gathered obsidian from their inventory.

Alex took out some flint and steel and started a fire to ignite the portal. Purple mist flew through the sky as they made their way back to the Overworld.

The first thing they saw when they walked out of the portal was a large red mushroom.

Steve looked out and saw water and then said, "We're on Mushroom Island."

"This is the same place where you had the building competition," added Kyra.

"Kyra, you're going to have to build us boats to get off the island," said Steve.

"Or we can go back to the Nether," suggested Alex.

Kyra didn't like that suggestion at all. She gathered wood and started to build boats for the group. As she looked through her inventory, she worried she might not have enough wood to build boats for everybody.

"Does anybody have wood I can use?" asked Kyra.

Everyone checked their inventory. Nobody had the resources to help Kyra build boats to get them off the island.

"Oh no," said Kyra, "we're stuck here. I better start chopping down trees or something."

"Maybe you can build a boat out of a mushroom," suggested Will.

"I don't think that will work," replied Kyra.

The group rested on the lawn. A mooshroom walked past, and they used a bucket to milk it and filled their food bar with mushroom stew.

As they ate and looked out at the water, the group was very despondent. They didn't want to be trapped on Mushroom Island. They needed to get to Henry, Lucy, and Max and save them from the rainbow griefers who had trapped them.

The gang began to chat, but Steve stood silently. He had an idea. Steve took out a potion of underwater breathing. He held it up in front of the group.

"Do you think this can help us get off the island?"

# 10
# UNDER THE SEA

Steve handed the potion to the others and they all drank.

"Okay, let's dive in!" Kyra said and they jumped into the water.

The group went deep into the blue ocean biome.

Steve wondered how long the potion would last and if they had enough to make it to the shore, but he also enjoyed exploring the ocean biome.

Kyra swam toward a structure deep within the ocean biome.

"It's an ocean monument," she called out to the group.

"I thought they were called ocean temples," said Will.

"I thought they were called water dungeons," said Steve.

It didn't matter what people called it—it was a large temple that grew on the very bottom of the ocean. Steve had never been in one, but he knew that squid-like creatures called the Guardian and the Elder Guardian guarded the temples, and they'd have to battle them to get anywhere near the gold treasure housed in these grand temples.

They approached the mammoth temple, lit by sea lantern blocks.

"Let's go in," said Alex as she swam toward the entrance.

Before Alex could enter, a Guardian made an incredibly loud noise and shot a dangerous laser beam at her. She avoided the beam, swimming away from the door.

Two more Guardians with piercing eyes emerged from the temple, swimming swiftly through the blue water. They omitted sounds as they shot laser beams at the group. Kyra took out her bow and arrow and shot at one of the Guardians.

"You got it!" said Steve, who also aimed an arrow at the underwater terror.

"I think we have to hit it a few more times," Kyra said.

The Guardian was fast, giving it an advantage in the water. No matter how hard they tried to swim faster, the water slowed down the group.

One of the Guardian's beams struck Steve; he lost hearts from his health bar. Steve felt wiped out. He'd never felt so exhausted in his life.

"What's happening?" he asked Alex.

"Don't worry, it's just mining fatigue. It will go away in a few minutes. Just make sure you hide from these Guardians. You don't want to get struck with a laser beam now," replied Alex.

The sound from the Guardians was deafening. They shot beams in all directions. Will was hit and also had mining fatigue.

Steve worried they would all get destroyed in the temple. He knew they'd respawn on the wheat farm, but he didn't want to start again. He had to battle these Guardians, get the gold treasure, and save his friends.

A Guardian swam past him with menacing eyes. Its tail moved quickly. Steve gathered the little energy he had left and struck it with a sword, clobbering the evil fish. The Guardian dropped prismarine crystals.

Alex and Will were in an intense battle with a sea of Guardians. She moved to avoid laser beams as Will shot as many arrows as he could at the mob. He destroyed one, but there were still four other Guardians attacking them. Steve swam toward them and shot arrows at the Guardians.

Kyra swam to join them, but was stopped by the Elder Guardian. The large fish had its creepy eye on her and shot an extremely powerful laser beam, striking her.

"Oh, I'm so tired." Kyra could barely get the words out as her health bar diminished rapidly.

"The Elder Guardian has the ability to give you serious mining fatigue. A lot more powerful than the smaller ones," Alex said and swam to Kyra's side.

Steve shot an arrow at the Elder Guardian as Will attacked a Guardian with his diamond sword.

"We'll never get in the temple," Kyra told Alex.

"We can't give up," Alex told her and then shielded Kyra from another laser beam as she shot an arrow at a Guardian.

Steve's battle with the Elder Guardian was one of the toughest he had experienced. He leapt at the evil creature with his diamond sword and with several strikes he was able to defeat this beast of the sea.

Will destroyed the final Guardian, and the group could finally make their way into the temple.

"We have to find the gold," Alex said as she walked through the massive temple.

"I have no idea where it could be," Steve said as he peeked through the empty rooms of the temple.

"I know we're going to see more Guardians soon. They live down here," Will told them, as he walked slowly, keeping a close look for any fish swimming in the temple.

It didn't take long. Two Guardians were swimming in the distance. The group tried to hide behind a temple wall, but the fish saw them.

The mobs' powerful, loud cry almost shook the temple as the group readied themselves for an attack. Each of them had their bow and arrow pointed in the direction of the creatures.

"Okay, go!" Alex screamed at them and they all shot arrows at the fish.

"We did it!" Kyra called out.

The group kept an eye out for more Guardians as they made their way farther into the underwater temple.

"Now I know why they also call this place a water dungeon. You can be trapped down here, deep within the ocean, fighting evil fish all day. It's awful. And it feels like there is nothing here," Will said as they peeked into a series of empty rooms.

"Patience," Alex told him. "We'll find treasure. If there weren't anything here, the Guardians wouldn't work so hard to protect it."

It felt like they were walking through the temple forever. Steve was certain the potion of underwater breathing would lose its effect at any minute.

"Look, sponges," Kyra pointed out. The group went into a room and extracted the sponges and placed them in their inventory.

They walked through a series of rooms but they were all empty.

"Maybe somebody beat us to the gold," Steve told them.

"There's just one hallway we didn't go down. We should look there," Alex told him.

"I'm worried we are wasting our time and our potion will wear out," said Steve.

The others didn't listen. They kept exploring, and when they reached the end of the tunnel, they found a room with a square of prismarine blocks.

"I bet the gold is under these prismarine blocks," said Steve.

Steve broke one of the blocks with a pickaxe and saw gold.

"Gold!" he shouted.

The others began to pickaxe the remaining blocks.

"Yes, all eight blocks are here," Alex said.

"Oh no!" Kyra called out.

The group didn't understand why Kyra was upset.

"Kyra, we just found gold," said Alex as she walked over the bricks and put them in her inventory.

Steve joined Alex, but when he picked up a gold brick, he saw a rainbow leg peeking out behind a block.

# 11
# MINING FATIGUE

The rainbow griefer shot an arrow at Steve, but missed. "Just take some gold and leave," Steve told the griefer.

"Like that will work," Kyra said and shot an arrow at the rainbow man.

Steve shot an arrow at the griefer and looked around for more rainbow griefers, but it looked as if this one was alone.

Alex and Will put as many bars of gold as they could in their inventory.

"Help us!" Steve shouted to Alex as he and Kyra battled the rainbow man, but she didn't listen and kept grabbing gold bars.

"Alex and Will, we need your help!" Kyra called to them.

The rainbow griefer leapt at Steve with a diamond sword and hit him.

Kyra shot an arrow at the griefer and quickly took her diamond sword from her inventory. She struck the rainbow griefer.

Alex took out her diamond sword and was about to strike the rainbow griefer, but the griefer screamed out, "Alex, this wasn't part of our plan!"

Steve was utterly shocked. "You know this griefer?"

"What plan?" Kyra asked as she hit the griefer.

"What are you planning to do to us?" Steve asked Alex.

Alex hit the rainbow griefer with her sword. "There's no plan. I can't be part of your dark world anymore."

"Alex, you promised. Stop!" the rainbow man pleaded as his health diminished from the blows.

"No, you've caused enough trouble.  Look at what the rainbow griefers have done to those poor treasure hunters in the desert. I can't work with you anymore. I don't think what you do is right," Alex said and delivered a final blow that destroyed the rainbow griefer, leaving Alex with all of his treasures.

"Here, you take his treasures." Alex handed around gold, iron ingots, and other items from the griefer.

"Alex, you're working with the rainbow griefers?" Steve was upset.

"Not all of them," she confessed. "Not the ones we fought in the cave."

"But the ones that trapped our best friends?" asked Steve sternly.

"I can explain," Alex told him.

"Explain? What were you planning to do with us once we got to the desert?" Kyra was mad.

"And what about you, Will?" asked Steve.

"Will really isn't part of this. He's innocent. And I'm not really part of the rainbow griefers, either," replied Alex.

"Really? Not part of the griefers? Then how did he know your name?" Steve was annoyed.

"I destroyed him, didn't I? Can't you see I'm with you guys now?" Alex tried to defend herself.

"How did you meet the rainbow griefers?" questioned Kyra.

"When you asked me to help and I said yes, one of the rainbow griefers saw me leaving the desert. He told me that if I brought your friends back here with their loot, he'd give me even more treasure." Alex felt a weight lift off her chest as she confessed.

"It's true. I heard it all," Will confirmed.

Steve didn't know who to believe anymore. But he also knew they were all on the bottom of the ocean and had very little time before the potion of underwater breathing lost its power. They had to make their escape. He had to trust Alex.

A sea of Guardians swam into the room with the gold bars, aiming laser beams at the group. They shot arrows, but they weren't destroying the sea creatures.

Steve felt weak. He looked at the others and could see they were also moving slower. The potion was losing its strength. They had to act fast. They shot more arrows and finally destroyed one Guardian.

"Yay!" Kyra exclaimed.

"We have more to destroy," Will reminded her as they shot more arrows and shielded themselves behind the gold bars.

The Guardians' beams were powerful and if any members of the group were hit, they might not survive. To escape, they continued shooting arrows.

Arrows flew through the water. The Guardians were getting weaker and finally they were destroyed, leaving a bunch of salmon. The group gathered the salmon and ate it. They needed their strength as they made their way to land.

As they attempted to exit the temple, an Elder Guardian swam past them. The group tried to hide, but it was pointless. Before it could omit a ray, Alex charged at the Elder Guardian and lashed out at it with her sword. She defeated the fish with a few hard strikes.

"Let's get out of here!" Steve shouted and they raced toward the door and through the calm blue water. Eventually, they looked up and saw land.

"We're going to make it!" Alex said as they got closer to the shore.

They walked onto the land and looked up.

"Oh no!" Will sighed when he saw the massive stone mountain that stood on the edge of the water. "There's no way we will be able to avoid climbing that stone mountain, is there?"

"No, but we've climbed mountains before, so we'll be fine," Steve reassured him.

"I've never climbed anything that high; it looks as if the peak touches the clouds." Will stared at the top of the mountain.

Kyra took out a potion of swiftness and was about to drink it when Steve stopped her.

"We can't go up the mountain too fast. We might fall off," Steve told her.

"Steve's right," said Alex. "It might be a large mountain, but we'll take it one step at a time and make it to the other side."

They walked along the gravel shoreline and made their way toward the mountain. Each step was hard, but they climbed carefully and were able to reach the top. Once they reached the mountain's peak, they stopped for a break.

"It's pretty up here." Kyra looked at the blue ocean and the sky.

Will stumbled and saw a hole in the middle of the mountain. "I think I see a cave."

"Oh, remember what happened last time we saw a cave by a mountain. It was filled with spiders and rainbow griefers," Kyra reminded him.

"Are there rainbow griefers here?" Steve asked Alex.

"I told you, I only knew the ones who approached me. It just happened that one of those rainbow griefers was in the ocean temple." Alex wanted them to believe her.

"Okay, we believe you," said Kyra.

Steve and the group walked into the cave.

"I don't see any rainbow griefers," Kyra said as she lit a torch and placed it on the wall.

"Steve!" a familiar voice called out.

"Kyra?" another, more distant voice exclaimed.

# 12
# A BLAST FROM THE PAST

"Adam?" Steve asked as he walked farther into the cave.

"Thomas?" Kyra asked.

"Yes," Adam walked toward them. "Thomas and I were here mining. I also need to get a bunch of resources to brew new potions."

Steve introduced his neighbors, Adam and Thomas, to Alex and Will. He hadn't seen Adam and Thomas in a long time. After Thomas created so much havoc in the village, he left the village with Adam and started to explore other biomes.

"We are on our way to save Henry, Max, and Lucy," Kyra told them. "They are trapped in a desert temple by rainbow griefers."

"We just encountered some rainbow griefers," Adam told them.

Steve didn't ask if Thomas had done any more griefing. Thomas had promised Steve he would never cause trouble again, and Steve wondered if he had stuck by his promise.

"Did you find any good minerals in this cave?" Kyra asked.

"We just got here; we were about to start mining. Want to join us?" asked Thomas.

"I think we have to go find our friends. We've had way too many detours already," replied Steve.

"Do you want us to join you?" asked Thomas.

"Seriously? That's a lot to ask of you." Steve was shocked. Thomas was the same person who blew up his wheat farm and told the entire village that Steve was the griefer, so Steve couldn't believe he wanted to help. Although, Thomas had helped rebuild everyone's homes and confessed to being the griefer, so maybe he was truly reformed.

"If you want to come, please join us," Steve said with a smile.

"Adam is an expert with potions," Kyra added.

"We want to mine first; we're low on resources," Adam told them.

This was a tough decision. They had to get to their friends and they also knew that traveling without the proper resources would put them at a disadvantage.

Steve and the gang took out their pickaxes and decided to mine with Adam and Thomas.

"Watch out!" Thomas called to Steve.

Steve looked down to see a large hole. "Thanks, if I fell down that hole, who knows where I'd end up."

The group began to mine. They dug deep within the ground until they reached a layer of diamonds.

"Diamonds!" Kyra was excited. They put the diamonds in their inventory.

Thomas dug his pickaxe into the ground and lava gushed out of the hole.

"Oh no!" Kyra cried. "Be careful, Thomas."

Lava began to flood the cave, and the group sprinted out of the cave as fast as they could. When they finally saw a light, they breathed a sigh of relief. They were safe.

"That was a close call," Steve said as they stood on the mountain.

"At least we were able to get some diamonds," said Kyra.

"It's getting dark. We have to find a place to build a shelter," Alex told them as she looked at the setting sun.

"Yes, that's a good idea. But we have to get down this mountain first," added Steve.

"There's a grassy area on the bottom of the mountain," Adam informed them. "We actually built a small house there. It's made out of wood, so it's not safe from creepers, but you're more than welcome to stay there."

The group trekked down the mountain toward Adam and Thomas's house.

The house was small but luckily they had enough beds for everybody. As they opened the door, a group of zombies came out from behind a tree. The green-headed, empty-eyed zombies crept toward the gang.

Steve shot an arrow at the zombies. The others joined him in an attack against these creatures of the night. The first zombies were defeated but more were approaching in the distance.

These new zombies were wearing armor. "They are going to be a lot harder to fight," Steve announced as he took out his diamond sword and leapt at the armored zombies. He struck one in an exposed area of skin and destroyed it. The group helped him battle the others, but they were surrounded.

Kyra destroyed another zombie with her sword. Alex and Will shot arrows at the others while Adam and Thomas battled the remaining zombies.

"There are more on the way!" Steve announced, seeing another horde of zombies walking toward the house.

They were trapped. They were outnumbered by zombies and there was no way they would be able to battle that many zombies.

Adam threw a potion of instant health two on the zombies and destroyed a group, but even with the diamond sword and the potions, the battle was too much for the group.

The new batch of zombies were just inches from them. Adam went to throw the potion on the zombies, but the bottle was empty.

"What are we going to do?" Adam asked.

"I don't know!" replied Kyra.

Steve destroyed two more zombies with his diamond sword, but there were too many to even count. When they began to lose all hope, the sun began to rise. The zombies burned. The group was safe. It was a new day.

# 13
# TREASURE HUNT

Adam and Thomas had been exploring the area for a long time and knew an easy way to get to the desert. "We just have to travel through the jungle and we'll be right near the desert biome," Adam told them as he showed them a map from his inventory.

"Steve and I were just in the jungle," Kyra told them. "We had to travel through the jungle to get to his building competition."

"Then you guys are jungle experts," said Adam. "Hopefully we will find a jungle temple."

The group walked through the grassy biome toward the tree-filled jungle.

Kyra saw a chicken in the distance and took out her bow and arrow. "Lunch," she told the group as she placed charcoal down and cooked the chicken.

"I see trees!" Will told them.

"Yes, we're almost at the jungle." Adam looked at his map.

Steve took out his shears. "The easiest way to get through the jungle is to make a path so we won't get lost in the trees."

When they reached the first patch of trees, Steve cleared a path for them.

"Guys, look—melons," Kyra said as she took out her pickaxe and cut away at the melon blocks to place in her inventory. The rest of the group followed.

Steve placed the last melon block in his inventory and asked, "How long will we be in the jungle? I want to get to the desert."

"This shouldn't take long. We'll be in the desert soon," Adam reassured him.

"I can't wait to see Henry, Max, and Lucy," said Kyra.

"I bet they'll be surprised to see us," added Thomas.

Steve and Kyra agreed.

Alex walked to the front of the group and then announced, "I see a pyramid!"

"A pyramid!" Kyra called out, "I've never seen a jungle pyramid."

"They're exceptionally rare," Steve told her.

"Is there treasure there?" asked Kyra.

"Yes, it's just like a jungle temple," Alex told her, as they sprinted toward the jungle pyramid.

Again Steve was reluctant to treasure hunt. They were almost at the desert and they had obtained so many treasures, they really didn't need any more, but he was outnumbered.

The group entered the pyramid, which was shaded with leaves. They searched the structure for treasure.

"Where's the treasure room?" asked Kyra as the group made their way through a series of empty rooms in the structure.

"Maybe somebody already emptied the pyramid," suggested Will.

"I heard there are usually diamonds in these pyramids," Alex said while searching every corner of the empty pyramid.

"Shh!" Steve told them, "I hear something."

"There are no hostile mobs here. It's daylight," Adam reassured him and continued to search the pyramid.

"Look!" Thomas shouted.

The group saw five rainbow griefers sprinting toward them.

"Alex, talk to them," demanded Steve.

"I told you I only know the ones who were trapping your friends. I don't know these guys. You have to believe me," pleaded Alex.

Steve took out his diamond sword and raced toward the group of griefers. Adam threw a potion of weakness on them, slowing the griefers down. Kyra shot arrows. Thomas, Will, and Alex sprinted at the griefers, striking them with their swords.

The griefers fought back, but they were too weak from Adam's potion and didn't have enough energy to win the battle. As each griefer was defeated, it dropped diamonds.

"They were the ones who emptied the treasure!" Kyra said as she and the others placed the fallen diamonds in their inventory.

"We have to get to the desert. I'm worried about Henry, Max, and Lucy," Steve told them as he walked toward the exit. The group followed him.

"It's just past these trees," said Adam.

Steve used his shears to make the path. They could see the sandy desert.

"See, we're almost there," Alex said as she walked in front of the group.

Steve wondered what she would do once she encountered the griefers she had promised to help. He had to believe Alex wouldn't turn on them. As they got closer to the sandy landscape—covered with cacti and dead bushes growing from the ground, known for being a hard place to survive—he mentally questioned Alex's motives.

The group stepped foot on sand. In the distance was a river.

"We're here!" Kyra said. "I know how to get to the desert temple from here. This isn't far from where the creeper attacked me."

The group had lost track of time and night was falling.

"We don't want to repeat the past," Steve said. "We need to find shelter or we might be attacked by a creeper, too."

Alex stopped walking, "Where's Will?"

The gang looked around, but Will was nowhere in sight.

Steve walked back a few feet and looked down. "There's a square hole!"

"He must have fallen in." Alex walked over to Steve.

"A desert dungeon," Adam said looking at the hole. "I'm sure of it."

"We have to jump in after him," said Kyra.

Kyra jumped into the hole, and the others followed. As Steve made his leap into the hole, he wondered if this was a trap.

# 14
# SWEET AS SUGAR

Although it was very dark, Steve could see a skeleton spawner in the center of the dungeon. Chests surrounded the spawner, and Steve knew that was where they'd find their treasure. But the dungeon was also filled with skeletons.

Will battled a skeleton, shooting arrows at the bony hostile mob. Steve placed a torch by the spawner to deactivate it, but the light from the torch didn't affect the skeletons that had already spawned. The group had to defeat the skeletons to survive.

*Clang! Bang!* Steve's diamond sword struck a skeleton. The skeletons fought back with their bows and arrows. The spawner had filled the small dungeon with skeletons and the group was outnumbered.

Adam threw a potion of healing at them and the skeletons began to lose energy.

The group forcefully attacked the undead mobs as they battled for their lives in this underground desert dungeon.

Kyra struck the final skeleton and the group gathered the bones dropped by the skeletons.

"Let's open the chest," Kyra said and the group gathered closely around her.

The first chest was filled with diamonds.

"We can make the most powerful sword in the world," Steve noted as he picked up a diamond. "I can't believe how many diamonds we've found so far."

"I know!" Alex said her inventory was full of diamonds.

"Of course, if the rainbow griefers defeat us, they get to keep all of our stuff," added Will.

"Don't worry, that won't happen," Alex told them.

"It better not," Steve told her.

The gang made their way from the dungeon and onto the sandy ground. Night was almost over.

"At least we found some shelter for the night," Steve joked.

"Night isn't over yet!" Alex called out as a creeper leapt toward her. She sprinted.

*Ka-boom!* The creeper exploded. Nobody was hurt, but this was a warning to the group that they weren't safe.

"Keep your eye out for hostile mobs. The sun didn't rise. We have to be ready for an attack," said Alex.

They didn't have to wait long for a hostile mob to attack them. A pair of red eyes crept toward them.

"A spider!" Kyra screamed and then leapt at the bug with her diamond sword.

"It has some friends," Steve said as two more spiders crawled toward them. Will and Alex slammed them with their swords.

The sun was rising. Steve sighed with relief.

"Where's the temple?" asked Steve.

"It's straight ahead," replied Kyra.

Adam looked at his map and confirmed they were going in the right direction. As they walked through the sparse desert, the gang stopped when they saw a patch of sugarcane. Steve took out his pickaxe and cut the lower part of the plant, dropping all the resources from the sugarcane.

The rest of the group gathered up all the sugarcane.

"We can use this to make paper," Kyra told them.

"And maps," added Adam.

"I always wanted to grow sugarcane on my wheat farm, but it isn't a good environment for it. I'm glad we found it here." Steve cut the last of the sugarcane blocks.

They could see the temple.

"Finally! We can save our friends," shouted Kyra.

Three large green cacti grew on the path to the temple.

"Watch out!" Will warned Kyra as she got close to the cacti. "If you get too close to the cacti, you will be harmed."

Kyra backed away. Nothing would stop her from saving her friends, especially a cactus. Kyra sprinted past the cacti and through the sand toward the temple.

She ran to the temple's entrance.

"I know where they're hiding them. I saw the bedrock room," Kyra said as she walked into the temple.

"I'm sure you do," a rainbow griefer said as he hit Kyra with his diamond sword.

# 15

# DUNES IN THE DESERT

teve shot an arrow at the rainbow griefer. Adam threw a splash potion of harming at the rainbow man. Kyra's energy was low, but she was able to strike him with her diamond sword.

"Where are our friends?" Kyra demanded, but the rainbow griefer wouldn't reply.

Another rainbow griefer emerged and Alex and Will sprinted toward it with their swords.

"Alex, what are you doing?" The griefer was shocked.

"You need to let those prisoners go. This isn't right," Alex said as she struck the rainbow griefer.

"Never!" he shouted back. Steve shot an arrow at the griefer. "You aren't going to get away with this."

Adam threw a potion of weakness at the griefer.

The griefer could barely get the words out, "Please, leave me alone. None of this was my idea."

"Who is in charge?" Steve demanded.

Will hit the griefer. "Tell us!"

"It's not me," replied the griefer.

Steve struck the griefer with his sword and he was destroyed.

When both of the griefers were defeated, and no treasures dropped, Steve and the gang knew that there must be more rainbow griefers holding the treasures and their friends.

The group walked into the desert temple.

"Henry, Max, Lucy!" Kyra called out.

"Shhh!" Steve warned her. "We don't want to announce to the rainbow griefers that we are here. We have to sneak in and save our friends."

Kyra apologized for shouting without thinking.

The group stopped when they saw the block of blue-stained clay in the middle of the room. They knew this was where the temple's treasure was housed. They also knew it was always booby-trapped.

"It looks like the treasure hasn't been touched." Steve inspected the treasure.

"Are you sure we're in the right temple?" asked Will.

Adam looked at his map. "I knew there was a temple here, but I can't say if it's the same temple where your friends are being trapped."

"Kyra, is this the temple?" asked Steve.

Kyra looked around. "I'm not sure."

"But what about the rainbow griefers?" asked Steve.

"Rainbow griefers are all over the desert," Alex told them.

"But one of those griefers knew you," said Steve.

"I just know the ones who approached me. Like the one we met in the underwater temple. Who knows who is holding your friends captive? There are so many rainbow griefers," said Alex.

Steve couldn't believe how many rainbow griefers they encountered. It seemed like the whole Minecraft world was crawling with these evil rainbow people.

"This has to be the temple," Kyra said as she walked around the first floor. "Aren't desert temples a rare find?"

"Well, if this is the right temple, we better start searching," Steve said and the group explored the sandstone temple.

"We should go to the lower level," suggested Kyra.

"But there's no light down there and hostile mobs can spawn," Thomas said. "Does everybody have enough energy to battle the griefers and hostile mobs?"

Adam took out a potion of strength. "Does anybody need this?"

"I think if we just eat the melons we found, we'll be fine. We need to save that potion; it will come in useful if we're attacked," said Alex.

The group ate melons and kept watch for rainbow griefers.

"I hear something," Steve said as he ate the melon.

The others were quiet, but they couldn't hear anything.

"We got you!" A rainbow griefer sprinted toward the middle of the desert temple and toward the TNT that booby-trapped the treasure.

Kyra shot an arrow at the griefer, but it didn't affect him at all. Adam threw a potion of weakness at him, but that didn't do much damage.

Steve guarded the blue clay block where the treasure was hidden and swung his sword at the griefer.

Thomas struck the griefer, "Where are our friends?"

"Alex, why don't you tell them?" The griefer looked at Alex, who was pointing her bow and arrow at the griefer.

"This is the griefer who approached me about bringing you guys here and stealing all your loot," she said.

"You traitor! You were supposed to be on our side. Why would you tell them about our plan?" The rainbow griefer was upset.

"I am not on your side anymore." Alex shot an arrow at the rainbow griefer. He finally succumbed to all the hits and was destroyed.

Steve could hear more voices. "I think there are more rainbow griefers heading our way. Get ready."

"I don't think it's a rainbow griefer," said Kyra.

The group heard a faint cry, "Help!"

"They're here!" Steve called out.

"But where?" asked Adam.

They took out their pickaxes and banged against the wall, but there was silence.

"Maybe we should try the other wall?" suggested Thomas.

The group split up. They banged deep into the sandstone walls, hoping their friends would be on the other side.

"Help!" the voices called out again.

"It's not coming from the other side of this wall," Steve told them. "I think they're underneath us."

The gang dug a hole in the ground with their pickaxes.

"Help!" the voices were getting louder.

The group dug as fast as they could. They wanted to get to their friends, who they now knew were trapped underneath the temple.

Steve and the gang fell through the big hole they had dug and landed underneath the floor of the temple.

Before Steve could light a torch, a spider jockey jumped at him. Steve swung at the spider with his sword, knocking the skeleton off the spider. Steve battled the skeleton while Thomas slayed the spider.

"Help!" the voices were very loud, and Steve wanted to destroy the skeleton as fast as he could. The others joined Steve and shot arrows at the skeleton.

"Help!" the voices cried.

"We're here!" Kyra called to them.

"Kyra?" Lucy called back. "Is that you?"

"Yes!" she screamed as she shot an arrow at the skeleton, "and I brought some friends with me."

The skeleton was destroyed. Kyra picked up the bone, and the group sprinted down the hall to their friends.

At the end of the hall was a bedrock wall.

"How are we going to break through this wall?" asked Will.

"Stand back. I have an idea." Steve began to build a cube of destruction.

# 16
# IT'S NOT A MIRAGE

**S**teve was crafting the cube of destruction with TNT when they heard the explosion.

*Boom!*

"Are you guys okay?" Steve called to them.

"Yes, but the side of the temple has fallen down, so we can escape," Henry shouted back at the gang.

"Meet us outside!" Lucy told them.

The group ran through the temple and onto the sandy desert ground.

"Lucy!" Kyra shouted and sprinted toward her.

"How are you guys?" Steve asked. "Are you hungry?"

"Adam and Thomas!" Max was shocked to see them.

Adam offered them potions that would help them regain their strength.

Henry, Lucy, and Max drank the potions.

"It was awful," explained Lucy. "They kept us trapped down there and didn't give us any food."

"I thought we'd never get out," confessed Henry. "I was really worried."

The reunion didn't last for long. Rainbow griefers rushed toward the temple.

The gang could hear them screaming at each other.

"You are the one who blew up the treasure," one rainbow griefer yelled at another.

The gang shielded themselves from the rainbow griefers, as they hid behind the temple.

"I don't think they see us," Henry told them.

"They're awful," added Lucy. "We have to get out of here fast."

"What about your treasure?" asked Kyra.

"They stole it all. We have nothing left, but I don't care. I just want to get out of the desert. We've been trapped here for days." Lucy was exhausted. Despite being a treasure hunter, she missed Steve's wheat farm.

"Do you see what I see?" Henry couldn't believe his eyes. Just a few feet away from them sat another desert temple. He thought it was a mirage, but it was real.

"How did we miss that?" asked Kyra.

The group made their way to the temple. They needed to escape from the rainbow griefers and they wanted to find treasure.

As the entered the temple, they quickly raced toward the blue clay block.

"Throw a bucket of water and we can slide down the hole once it's activated," Henry told the group.

Will was about to break the blue clay block when Steve shouted, "Don't break it!"

Steve began to break the orange clay block and jumped through the hole.

The rest of the group slid down to meet Steve by the four chests that contained the treasure.

"Don't step on the pressure plate!" Henry yelled over at Alex, who stood very close to the dangerous plate.

Steve opened the first chest and found diamonds and gold.

Max opened the second chest and found rotten flesh and iron and gold.

"Yuck," Kyra said when she saw the rotten flesh.

"I'm opening this one. Hope it's not stinky," said Alex as she opened the third chest, which was filled with golden horse armor and saddles. She offered the saddles to everyone in the group.

Henry opened the final chest, which contained an enchantment book. "Adam, you'll love this book because you're a potion expert."

The group placed the treasures in their inventory and were ready to make their way back to the wheat farm when they heard a noise in the temple.

"Oh no!" Kyra said. "More rainbow men!"

Four rainbow men sprinted in. One of the rainbow men stood in front of Steve and said, "Looks like you guys got that treasure."

"Good job, Alex. You got their friends here," the second rainbow griefer told her.

"Now give us all of your stuff," demanded the third griefer.

The fourth rainbow griefer said, "Don't trust Alex. She is with them now."

"What?" The first rainbow griefer was shocked. "Why? Don't you want all their treasures? They are fools."

"They aren't fools," Alex defended her friends. "And I don't want their treasure. I just want their friendship. I also want evil people like you to stop terrorizing innocent people."

The rainbow griefers laughed at Alex and then sprinted toward the group with their diamond swords.

"It's a battle to the death!" one of the rainbow griefers said as he struck Steve with his sword.

Adam was running low on potions. He splashed them with a potion of weakness, but he didn't have enough potion to make an impact on the griefers. They were still able to battle with full energy.

Kyra tried to get out her bow and arrow but she wasn't fast enough.

"Ouch!" she cried as two rainbow griefers struck her with swords.

Max came up from behind the rainbow griefers that attacked Kyra and clobbered them with his diamond sword.

Dusk was setting, and a creeper silently passed by the desert temple. It was too late to move when they heard it tick and ignite.

*Ka-Boom!*

Two rainbow griefers were destroyed.

"Oh no!" Kyra pointed to the griefers who had been destroyed. "Alex and Will were fighting them when the creeper exploded."

The creeper also destroyed Alex and Will. The group was upset, but they had to fight the remaining two griefers.

Steve swung his diamond sword at the rainbow griefer. Thomas shot an arrow. Adam threw potion at another griefer. Henry, Max, and Lucy also struck the griefers with their swords. The evil griefers were outnumbered and lost the battle.

"I can't believe that creeper destroyed Alex and Will." Kyra was really upset.

Steve wanted to tell her that it was okay, they'd respawn at the wheat farm, but then he realized that wasn't the last place they slept.

"They will respawn in Adam's house. I hope they can find their way from there," Steve told her.

"Should we head over to my place near the mountain?" asked Adam. "We can meet them there."

"Should we even trust Alex? She did confess to working with the griefers," Kyra told them.

Before anyone could talk, Alex and Will appeared in front of them.

"We wanted to help you win this battle," said Alex.

"How did you get here?" asked Steve.

"We teleported," Alex told them.

Alex took out her diamond sword and said, "We have some rainbow griefers to destroy. I know the griefer who is behind all of this and we have to find him."

# 17
# TREASURES AND TROUBLES

Alex sprinted toward a wooden house in the middle of the desert. "This is where the head rainbow griefer lives."

The griefers could be seen through the window of the wooden house.

"Shh!" Steve said as he looked in the window.

"I can throw a potion on them," suggested Adam.

"We need a plan," Steve told Alex. "We can't just sprint in and destroy them without a strategy."

"Okay." Adam started to propose a plan, but was cut short when a griefer shot an arrow at the group.

Adam told his friends to take off their armor.

"Seriously? Now?" Lucy couldn't believe it.

"Yes, trust me. I have a plan," Adam told his friends.

Adam only had a few drops left of the potion, but he tossed whatever he could from the potion of weakness bottle at the griefers.

He then splashed a potion of invisibility on his friends and the griefers stopped in their tracks.

"Where are they?" the head rainbow griefer—who wore a black helmet—asked the four rainbow griefers who stood next to him.

"Why are we moving so slowly?" asked another.

"They have an alchemist with them. Don't worry, the effects won't last very long. We'll find them soon. But for now, just shoot arrows in their direction," the head griefer instructed his band of griefers.

"What direction is that?" asked one of the griefers.

"Over there!" the head griefer commanded. "Where we saw them last."

The rainbow griefers blindly shot arrows at where they thought the gang was standing.

"I don't think we're hitting anyone," one of the rainbow griefers said as he was struck with an arrow from an invisible Steve.

Lucy sprinted toward the head rainbow griefer and struck him with her diamond sword. "That's for trapping us!"

Kyra stood next to Lucy and also hit the head rainbow griefer with a powerful blow from her sword.

The head rainbow griefer's health was diminishing. "Help!" he called to the other rainbow griefers.

The rainbow griefers tried to attack Lucy and Kyra, but every time they struck their swords, it didn't seem to hit anybody.

"It's too hard! We can't see them!" The rainbow griefers were fighting air; it was an impossible battle. A barrage of arrows flew at them.

Adam knew they had to work fast. The potion didn't last too long and they needed to damage the rainbow griefers if they wanted to have any advantage. Adam sprinted toward the group of griefers, striking as many as he could with his sword. The others joined him.

If someone was to walk by and watch the battle, it would appear almost comical, as the rainbow griefers awkwardly fought an invisible enemy.

"Stop! I surrender!" the head rainbow griefer shouted, and his fellow griefers looked on in shock and horror.

"What?" one screamed out, losing a life when a diamond sword struck his stomach. "There's no surrendering."

"That's right," Henry said as he hit the head griefer with a final blow.

"We won!" Lucy shouted.

"Not yet," Steve said as he watched his friends lose their invisibility and get struck by the remaining rainbow griefers.

The griefers were losing energy; they had been hit too many times to fight properly. One griefer was able to escape, sprinting from the battle. Kyra shot an arrow at him, but it didn't hit him. He was gone. The other three griefers stayed to battle. They used all their might to fight the gang.

Max, Henry, and Thomas struck one of the griefers until he was destroyed. Kyra shot a final arrow at another griefer and he was defeated. There was only one griefer left.

"Stop," he pleaded.

The group stopped. It was an unfair battle. There were nine in their group and only one griefer left.

"Why did you steal all of our stuff?" asked Henry.

"It wasn't my idea," he defended himself.

"But it was wrong. Why would you listen to some-one who attacks innocent people?" Lucy was upset.

"I was just following orders," the griefer replied.

"You have to think for yourself," Alex told him. "I used to work for that rainbow griefer, but I realized that it was wrong. You don't follow people who are only out to hurt others."

"Please let me go," he begged.

"Why should we?" asked Henry.

"Because I'm innocent," he said with a whimper.

"Innocent?" Alex was annoyed. "Didn't you hear what I just said? When you follow bad people, you aren't innocent."

"Do you promise not to attack anyone and to leave this gang of rainbow griefers?" Thomas asked him.

"Yes," he replied.

"We will let you go if you give back any treasures you have taken from my friends," said Thomas.

"I don't have anything," the rainbow griefer confessed.

"Wow, you were fighting us for nothing?" Alex was dumbfounded.

Henry looked through the windows of the wooden house and saw a chest. "I think all of the treasure is here. Come in and help us open this chest."

They followed the griefer into the house.

"Open it. I want to make sure it isn't booby-trapped," Henry demanded.

The group stood back. They feared the chest was trapped and the floor would open up and they'd be thrown into a lava pit. As the griefer lifted the cover of the chest, the gang held their breath. They were nervous.

The griefer slowly opened the chest, revealing all of the treasures Henry, Max, Lucy, and Kyra had found on their treasure hunt. It wasn't a trap! It was a victory! They were excited!

"It's all here," said Henry.

"Yes, look at all of our diamonds!" Lucy looked down at the lost treasure.

Henry gathered the treasure. He handed a portion of the treasure to Max, Lucy, and Kyra.

"We're going to let you go," Henry said as he pointed his diamond sword in the direction of the griefer. "But we better not see you ever again."

"I promise. Thank you," replied the griefer.

"Are you also going to promise to stop following bad people and only do what you think is right?" asked Thomas.

"Yes, I will," the griefer said.

The group went outside to see him off and he sprinted away as night set in.

The group could make out a creeper off in the distance. The rainbow griefer was headed in his direction.

*Ka-boom!*

"Oh no!" Kyra shouted.

"When he respawns with his fellow rainbow griefers, I hope he'll remember to make his own decisions," said Henry.

"It's almost night," Steve told the group. "We have to find a place to sleep."

"We can stay in the desert temple. All we have to do is make beds," suggested Alex.

The group walked toward the temple, but two Endermen crept past holding bricks of sand.

Henry accidently stared at one, and its mouth gaped open as it teleported toward Henry.

Adam threw a splash potion at the Endermen and they teleported away.

"Quick, get in the desert temple. We can build a wall at the entrance so the Endermen can't get in," said Alex.

As they sprinted toward the temple, the Endermen teleported back toward the group.

"Lead them to the river!" Kyra suggested.

Steve and Henry sprinted in the direction of the river and the Endermen followed closely behind.

"I hope we'll make it," Henry looked back.

Steve jumped in the water and Henry followed. Luckily so did the Endermen.

Steve made his way out of the water, avoiding the cacti lining the water's edge.

"We need to get back to the temple," Henry said and the two sprinted.

Alex was almost done constructing the door. Henry and Steve took out their pickaxes.

"Stop!" Alex shouted. "I left a hole for you guys. Don't destroy the door!"

They made their way through the small hole. The group had made beds for everybody, including Steve and Henry. When the door was finished, they all were relieved. It was dark and they wanted to sleep.

# 18
# REWARDS

It was dawn and the group awoke in the desert temple.

"I think we should head home," Steve told the group.

"Whose home?" Alex asked. "We don't live on the wheat farm."

"Would you like to come back to the wheat farm?" Steve asked Alex.

"I think it's time for Will and me to go back to our home," said Alex.

Steve looked at Adam and Thomas.

"It's probably best if we stay away from the village for a bit longer. After everything I did to the village, I feel like we need to find another place to live." Thomas looked at Adam as he spoke.

"I'd love to go back to the village, but Thomas is right, we should wait," confirmed Adam.

"What about you guys?" Steve looked at Max, Lucy, Kyra, and Henry.

Steve was surprised at their response: the treasure hunters were exhausted and they wanted to spend some-time on the wheat farm to recharge.

"I want to see Jasmine," confessed Lucy.

"I want to trade all of my emeralds and diamonds at Eliot the Blacksmith's shop and craft a bunch of powerful swords at your house," said Henry.

"I need to check on my house," said Kyra.

"I want to relax and eat carrots and potatoes," said Max.

The group said their goodbyes to their old friends Adam and Thomas and their new friends Alex and Will.

"I hope we'll see you all again soon," said Steve.

The new and old friends all said the same. Steve and his friends made their way back to the wheat farm.

Henry looked at the map and led the group toward the jungle. Steve looked at the green leaves that touched the sky. He knew the journey home wouldn't be easy, but he had his friends with him.

The paths of the jungle were dense with trees. Steve thought he saw a rainbow griefer sprint past them, but was relieved to see it was only a wild ocelot. Henry held out some raw fish, ready to tame the cat.

There would be a new pet at the wheat farm.

The cat purred as it followed the gang home.

# ALSO AVAILABLE FROM SKY PONY PRESS

## The Quest for the Diamond Sword

### An Unofficial Gamer's Adventure, Book One

by Winter Morgan

Steve lives on a wheat farm and likes to spend his mornings in the village and trade his wheat for emeralds, armor, books, swords, and food. One morning, he finds that zombies have attacked the villagers. The zombies have also turned the village blacksmith into a zombie, leaving Steve without a place to get swords. To protect himself and the few villagers that remain, Steve goes on a quest to mine for forty diamonds, which are the most powerful mineral in the Overworld. He wants to craft these diamonds into a diamond sword to shield him and the villagers from the zombies.

Far from his home, with night about to set in, Steve fears for his life. Nighttime is when users are most vulnerable in Minecraft. As he looks for shelter in a temple, he meets a trio of treasure hunters, Max, Lucy, and Henry, who are trying to unearth the treasure under the temple. Steve tells them of his master plan to mine for the most powerful mineral in the Overworld—the diamond. The treasure hunters are eager to join him. Facing treacherous mining conditions, a thunderstorm, and attacks from hostile mobs, these four friends question if it's better to be a single player than a multiplayer as they try to watch out for each other and chase Steve's dream at the same time.

Will Steve find the diamonds? Will his friends help or hinder the search? Should he trust his new treasure hunter friends? And will Steve get back in time to save the villagers?

$7.99 paperback • ISBN 978-1-63220-442-4

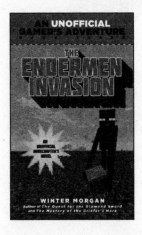

# ALSO AVAILABLE FROM SKY PONY PRESS

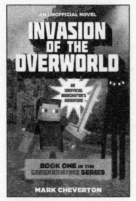

**Invasion of the Overworld**

**Book One in the Gameknight999 Series: An Unofficial Minecrafter's Adventure**

by Mark Cheverton

Gameknight999 loved Minecraft. He reveled in building structures, playing on servers, creating custom maps, and more. But above all else, he loved to grief—to intentionally ruin the gaming experience for other users. As the self-proclaimed "King of the Griefers," Gameknight played the game for himself at the expense of everyone else, keeping the list of his friends in the game short.

But when one of his father's inventions teleports him into the game, Gameknight is forced to live out a real-life adventure inside the digital world of Minecraft. What will happen if he's killed in the game? Will he respawn? Disconnect? Die in real life? Unsure, Gameknight must play the game with all of his skill and knowledge. He has to stay one step ahead of the sharp claws of zombies and pointed fangs of spiders. Eventually, he discovers the best-kept secret about Minecraft, something not even the game's programmers realize: the creatures within the game are alive!

This action-packed homage to the worldwide computer game phenomenon is a runaway publishing smash and the perfect companion for Minecraft fans of all ages.

$9.99 paperback • ISBN 978-1-63220-711-1

# ALSO AVAILABLE FROM SKY PONY PRESS

## Battle for the Nether

**Book Two in the Gameknight999 Series: An Unofficial Minecrafter's Adventure**

by Mark Cheverton

As *Invasion of the Overworld* ends, Gameknight999 and his friend Crafter find themselves on a new Minecraft server. Knowing the lives of all those within Minecraft—as well as those in the physical world—are depending on them, Gameknight and Crafter will need to search the land to recruit an NPC army if they are to stand a fighting chance.

Malacoda is the King of the Nether, a terrible ghast that has a vile, evil plan for the destruction of Minecraft. His massive army includes blazes, magma cubes, zombie pigmen, and wither skeletons, and his plans will take one of Gameknight's closest friends from him. Gameknight999 will have to sift through the chaos and put his Minecraft-playing skills to the test to solve the mysterious disappearance of all the crafters. But the battles Gameknight fought on the previous server and the enemy he faced have left him doubting his strength and his knowledge, and he'll need to reach deep inside himself to summon all the courage he has if he's to have any shot at victory.

Epic battles, terrible monsters, heartwarming friendships, and spine-tingling suspense . . . *Battle for the Nether* takes the adventures of Gameknight999 to the next level in a nonstop roller-coaster ride of adventure.

$9.99 paperback • ISBN 978-1-63220-712-8